P9-EFJ-467

THE NOTEBOOK OF DOOM

RISE OF THE BALLOON GOONS

by Troy Cummings

SCHOLASTIC INC.

Read more books in

THE NOTEBOOK OF DOOM series!

#1

#2

#3

#4

TABLE OF CONTENTS

To Penny and Harvey: Stay out of trouble.

Thank you, Katie Carella and Liz Herzog, for taking my ideas and making them better.

If you purchased this book without a cover, you should be aware that this book is stolen property. It was reported as "unsold and destroyed" to the publisher, and neither the author nor the publisher has received any payment for this "stripped book."

No part of this work may be reproduced, stored in a retrieval system, or transmitted in any form or by any means, electronic, mechanical, photocopying, recording, or otherwise, without written permission of the publisher. For information regarding permission, write to Scholastic Inc., Attention: Permissions Department, 557 Broadway, New York, NY 10012.

Library of Congress Cataloging-in-Publication Data

Cummings, Troy.
Rise of the balloon goons / by Troy Cummings.
p. cm. – (The Notebook of Doom ; 1)
Summary: Alexander has just moved into Stermont, but the elementary school is being torn down, his new classroom is located in the hospital morgue, a notebook he finds is full of information about monsters–and everywhere he turns there are spooky balloon men determined to attack him.
ISBN 978-0-545-49323-9 (pbk.) — ISBN 978-0-545-49322-2 (hardback) — ISBN 978-0-545-49326-0 (ebook)
1. Monsters—Juvenile fiction. 2. Novelty balloons—Juvenile fiction. 3. Elementary schools—Juvenile fiction. 4. Horror tales. [1. Monsters—Fiction. 2. Novelty balloons—Fiction. 3. Elementary schools—Fiction. 4. Schools—Fiction. 5. Horror stories.]
I. Title.
PZ7.C91494Ris 2013
[E]–dc23
2012034520

ISBN 978-0-545-49322-2 (hardcover) / ISBN 978-0-545-49323-9 (paperback)

Copyright © 2013 by Troy Cummings
All rights reserved. Published by Scholastic Inc.
SCHOLASTIC, BRANCHES, and associated logos are trademarks and/or registered trademarks of Scholastic Inc.

12 11 10 9 8 7 6 5 4 3 2 1 13 14 15 16 17 18/0

Printed in China 38
First Scholastic printing, July 2013

Book design by Liz Herzog

CHAPTER 1 STERMONT

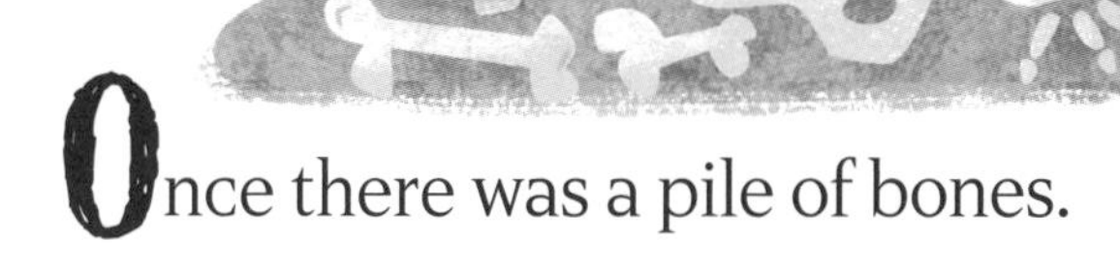

Once there was a pile of bones.

Actually, the bones weren't in a pile. They made up a small skeleton, which was filled with squishy guts. On top of that skeleton sat a huge skull with deep eye sockets. These eye sockets held a pair of googly eyes.

The whole thing would have been really gross, except it was covered in a layer of skin and had a mop of curly hair on top. This mop-haired, bug-eyed, gut-filled bag of bones was named Alexander Bopp. And he was scared to death.

Alexander was scared of:

1. spending his first night in a new house;
2. going to a new school in a new town; and
3. having to make new friends.

Alexander rolled over on his air mattress and looked out the window. The moon lit up a row of rooftops, behind which stood a water tower that said STERMONT. Alexander's new home.

CHAPTER 2 FRIGHT AND EARLY

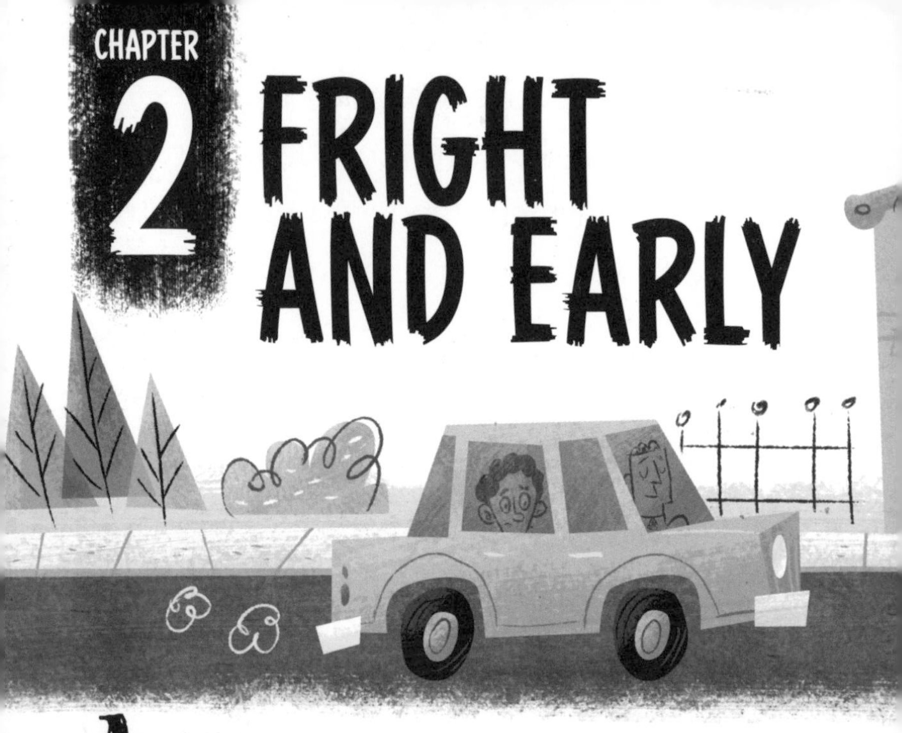

Alexander's dad drove slowly down Main Street. "I'll look on this side, and you look on that side. This town must have a breakfast place."

Alexander looked out his window. They passed a park, a bank, a comic-book shop . . . and then someone dancing like crazy on the sidewalk. Wait, it wasn't a person. It was one of those bendy balloon guys that businesses put out to attract customers. It was yellow, and it was

wiggling beside a sign that said **NOW SERVING BREAKFAST!**

"Hey, Dad," Alexander said. "Here's a place."

They parked next to the dancing balloon guy.

SMACK!

"Whoa!" Alexander jumped in his seat. The balloon guy had flopped right onto the windshield. It snapped back up and continued to dance.

Alexander's dad shook his head. "You're jumpy today, Al. That's just a big bag of air."

"I know," said Alexander, uncovering his eyes.

"In fact," said his dad, "we should be happy to see this goony-balloony. Otherwise we might have missed this diner." He made a dopey face and wiggled his fingers at the balloon figure. "Thanks, balloon goon!"

Alexander smiled. Then he walked the long way around the balloon and into the diner.

CHAPTER 3 MAP OUT OF IT!

The door chimed as Alexander and his dad left the diner. "Were those great pancakes, or what?" his dad asked.

Alexander didn't answer. He was studying his paper place mat: a map of Stermont, laid out like a maze.

"Hey, neat," said his dad. "Maybe we could take extras to hand out at your party."

Alexander poked his nose over the map. "Party?"

"Sure!" said his dad. "Your birthday party!"

"But, Dad," Alexander grumbled, "I don't want a party. I don't even *have* a real birthday this year."

"But that's the best part about a leap-year

birthday, Al," said his dad. "February twenty-ninth only comes around once every four years. So we get to *choose* your birthday this year. And I choose tomorrow!"

Alexander frowned.

"Besides," his dad continued, "I already made the party invitations." He stuffed a stack of envelopes into Alexander's backpack. "Pass 'em out to your new classmates today!"

Alexander followed his dad toward their car. Way down the street, he could make out a wiggly shape in front of a bank — another dancing balloon guy. This one was purple.

"Hey," said Alexander. "There's another" — he looked around — "wait . . . where's *our* balloon goon? It was right here when we parked. . . ."

"Hmmm?" said his dad. He was fishing around for his keys. "I dunno. Maybe someone moved it." He unlocked the car. "Hop in, Al!"

Alexander tried to yank open his door, but then — **CRUNCH!** — it scraped against the curb. "Huh?" he said. The car was lower to the ground than before.

"Dad! This tire's flat."

"No problemo," said his dad. "We'll just pop on the spare and — wait a minute! *This* tire's flat, too." He rubbed his chin.

Alexander took a step back. "Uh, Dad. All *four* tires are flat."

"That's strange," said his dad. "Maybe there's glass on the road. . . ."

Alexander looked across the street: two more cars with flat tires. *Something weird is going on here*, he thought.

His dad stood up and brushed off his pants. "Sorry, Al. I have to call a tow truck. Do you think you could walk to school?"

Alexander's eyes widened. "By myself?"

"Sure, kiddo!" His dad smiled. "Here — pass me that place-mat maze."

His dad spread out the place mat on the hood of the car and pulled a pen from his pocket.

"See — we're here," he said, circling the diner. "And your new school is right there."

He drew a path through the maze. “You head down Main Street and — oops, dead end! Turn left and then north and then — oh! We got stuck in the glue factory! Wait, wait. So you loop back — oh, wow! This town has three graveyards! And then you go past that bakery. And bingo! You’re at school!”

Alexander gulped. *My first day in a new town,* he thought. *And I'm walking myself to school.*

"Now go make friends. Then tomorrow we'll have a birthday blowout! High five!"

Alexander gave his father a medium five. Then he followed his place-mat maze down Main Street.

CHAPTER 4

ONE-TWO PUNCH!

Alexander soon found himself at Stermont Elementary. There was no one else around. *I must be late*, he thought.

He headed toward the door — but then froze. Two balloon goons were wobbling there — one blue and one green.

Alexander took a big deep breath. As he stepped between the balloons, he saw words printed on them. The blue balloon said PARDON, and the green one said OUR DUST. Alexander looked down but didn't see any dust.

There was a tug on his backpack. He looked over his shoulder and saw a flappy blue arm tangled in the straps.

Alexander untwisted the wiggling arm and turned to see . . .

. . . the green balloon goon's big, ugly face!

"Whoa!" Alexander shouted. The goon's nose pressed right up against Alexander's.

Then — **FOOMP!** Alexander was clobbered on the head, from behind. It felt like he'd been socked by a boxing glove. He spun around just in time to be hit in the face. **FOOMP!** Alexander stumbled and fell backward.

Both balloons leaned over Alexander, grinning. Their long, wobbly arms swooped in and grabbed at his jacket. Alexander tried to kick them away, but the green one wrapped its arm around his ankle. Alexander's shoe came off as he tried to wriggle free.

A loud crashing sound came from inside the school. The balloon goons instantly let go of Alexander. They snapped upright.

Alexander scrambled to his feet and ran into the school. His heart was pounding as he yanked the door shut behind him.

CHAPTER 5

A TON OF BRICKS

Alexander stood inside, catching his breath. The school was perfectly quiet, and all the lights were off. Daylight came in through the door behind Alexander, casting long shadows down the hallway.

"Hello?" he called out.

"Hello?" said his echo.

Alexander clutched the straps on his backpack and started down the dim hallway. He passed several classrooms, all empty.

"Anyone there?"

Alexander tripped over something brown with white stitches. *A flat football* . . . he thought.

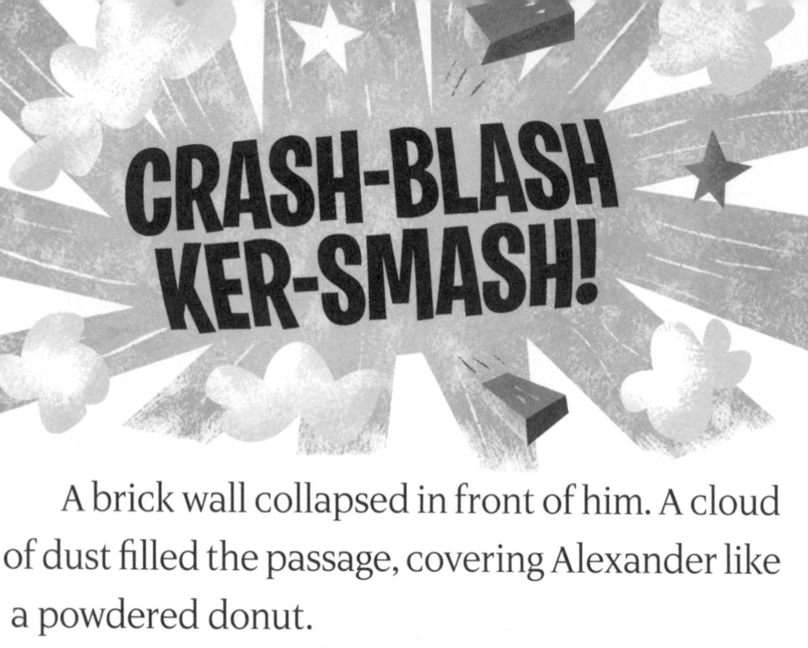

A brick wall collapsed in front of him. A cloud of dust filled the passage, covering Alexander like a powdered donut.

Alexander looked through the broken wall and saw a giant yellow claw — a wrecking crane!

He *had* to get out of there. He climbed over the smashed bricks, which was tricky with just one shoe. Then he spotted something rectangular in the rubble, wrapped in a dusty scarf.

Alexander unwrapped the object. It was an old notebook.

He flipped to a page in the middle.

PLAYING MANTIS

A huge green bug monster. About as tall as a giraffe (minus the neck).

HABITAT All playgrounds — at schools, public parks, etc.

DIET Regular-size bugs. (They spit out the shells.)

BEHAVIOR These giant bugs love playground equipment, but they play too rough. If you notice a dent in the slide or see a swing with one chain shorter than the other, then there's likely a mantis nearby.

WARNING! The only way to avoid a playing mantis is to sit quietly against the wall during recess.

Alexander shivered. He thumbed through the book and saw page after page of monster drawings.

"HEY!" a voice shouted from down the hall.

Alexander stuffed the notebook into his backpack.

A woman was storming toward Alexander. She wore a gray shirt, gray pants, gray shoes, and gray glasses. Her hair was in a long braid, coiled on top of her head like a snake.

"Why are you playing in a construction site?!" she demanded.

"I wasn't playing! This is my school. I'm a

new kid! But nobody was here and then the wall crashed and —"

"This school was closed to deal with —" The woman looked at Alexander.

"Well, this is a dangerous building," she continued. "Even a 'new kid' should have been able to read the warning sign out front."

"Do you mean the big 'Pardon Our Dust' balloons?"

"Balloons?" asked the woman. "No. There's a big 'Danger! Keep Out!' sign, Alexander."

Alexander blinked. "How did you know my name?"

The woman smiled. Actually, she didn't smile; she just frowned less. "We've been expecting you. Only we expected you at the *right* building. Not the one being torn down."

Alexander pulled out his map. "But it says here —"

The woman snatched the map away. "This place mat is outdated! We've moved the school while they finish construction." She reached into the coils of her braid and pulled out a marker.

"You're here," she said, circling the school. "And your new school is . . . here." Ignoring the maze, she drew a line that cut through someone's backyard and a funeral home, ending at **STERMONT GENERAL HOSPITAL**.

She handed the map to Alexander. "Now get to school, before your principal gets angry."

"My principal?" asked Alexander.

The woman knelt down. Her ID badge dangled before Alexander's eyes.

Ms. Vanderpants waved for Alexander to get moving. So he did.

CHAPTER 6 GOING DOWN!

Alexander looked up at the hospital. Right away, he noticed how *this* Stermont Elementary was better than the other one:

1. The lights were on.
2. It hadn't been knocked over by bulldozers.

A man sat at the front desk, writing on a clipboard. He had frizzy white hair that stood straight up. Alexander read the nameplate on the desk.

MR. HOARSELY
SECRETARY

"Excuse me," said Alexander.

"Eep!" Mr. Hoarsely said. "You scared me!"

"Sorry," said Alexander. "I'm new here, and, uh . . ."

"Oh, you must be *Alexander*."

Mr. Hoarsely checked his clipboard. "Well, look at that . . . happy sort-of-birthday."

He checked his watch. His eyebrows shot up. "You're late! And filthy! And why are you only wearing one shoe?"

"Stermont Elementary students *must* wear both shoes at all times — school policy!" said Mr. Hoarsely. He pulled a pair of green galoshes out of the Lost & Found. "Quick — put these on before the principal sees you!"

Alexander took the galoshes. They looked like little froggies.

"I can't wear these!" he said.

"Ms. Vanderpants will flip if she sees a sock-footed student!" said Mr. Hoarsely.

Alexander made a sour face and pulled just the left galosh over his sock.

"Perfect. Now, let's find your class," said Mr. Hoarsely, checking his clipboard. "Sixth graders are in the Emergency Room.... Kindergartners are in Brain Surgery.... Ah — here you are!"

He pointed to the elevators. "Press **M** to get to your classroom."

Alexander stepped into the elevator and pressed **M**.

The elevator went down several floors and then opened. Alexander read the sign on the wall:

MORGUE →

Morgue? thought Alexander, stepping out of the elevator. *But that's where hospitals keep dead bodies!*

CHAPTER 7

THE MORGUE THE MERRIER

Alexander tugged open the big metal door and peeked into a cold, windowless room.

The walls were lined with little square doors. Most of the doors were open, with long metal slabs sticking out like tables. Alexander's new classmates were using these slabs as desks. The class grew silent as Alexander stepped into the room.

"WHO DARES ENTER THE FORBIDDEN CHAMBER?" boomed a loud voice.

One of the square doors in the back of the room shuddered and then burst open.

"AHHH!" Alexander screamed.

A grinning man had popped out of the hatch. "Ha! Just kidding! Welcome! I'm Mr. Plunkett!" He wore a pink-and-orange flowery shirt, green pants, and purple shoes.

Mr. Plunkett wrote **ALEXANDER BOPP** on the board. Then he plopped a pointy hat onto Alexander's head. "Why don't you introduce yourself?"

"Um, hi, I'm new and it's great to meet you and my dad is a dentist and we just moved to Stermont yesterday and, um —" Alexander said, way too fast.

The classroom door swung open with a big jerk. Rip Bonkowski barged into the room.

"Who's the weenie?" Rip asked, staring at Alexander.

"Now, Rip," said Mr. Plunkett. "Is it a good idea to call someone a 'weenie'?"

Mr. Plunkett turned to the class. "Remember what we talked about in our writing unit! You can call *anyone* a weenie — so boring!" He winked at Alexander. "If you're going to give someone a nickname, make it count!"

Alexander's mouth dropped open.

"Let's see. . . ." Mr. Plunkett studied Alexander. "Notice his silly frog boot. This guy clearly loves slimy green things!"

He crossed out Alexander's name and wrote **SALAMANDER SNOTT** beneath it.

"There!" he said.

The class broke into laughter.

Alexander tore off his hat. "Unbelievable!" he snapped. Everyone stopped laughing. "A lousy nickname already? This whole day has been a joke!" Alexander gritted his teeth. "I've been lost, yelled at, crushed by bricks — and attacked by monsters!" He held his hands up like claws. "Huge, ugly, terrible, walking balloon goons!"

Everyone gasped. Then they laughed even harder. Except for a hoodie-wearing kid in the back row. He or she scribbled something in his or her notebook.

"Oh, Salamander," Mr. Plunkett said through tears of laughter, "you are one *funny* fella!"

Alexander shook his head. *Why did I just tell everyone about the balloon goons?* he thought. *Good thing I didn't mention the monster notebook!*

"Speaking of funny," said Mr. Plunkett, "I'd like to discuss a little prank I found on my seat." His eyebrows lowered.

Mr. Plunkett slapped a deflated whoopee cushion on his desk.

"A *flat* whoopee cushion is no joke," he said. "Next time, fill it with air!"

WHOOPEE!

RRRIINNGG!

The class rushed past Alexander. *Finally, lunch! This day is bound to get better*, he thought. *Right?*

CHAPTER 8 SPILLED MILK

Alexander took the elevator to the cafeteria. **DING!** The doors slid open.

FOOMP! Alexander was hit in the face with a dodgeball.

"Gotcha, Salamander!" said Rip.

The ball landed with a thud at Alexander's feet.

"Oh, man! It's flat," Rip said. "I was hoping to bounce it off your nose!"

"Ripley Bonkowski!" came a voice from around the corner.

"Uh-oh," said Rip.

Ms. Vanderpants thundered into view.

"Alexander," she said, "I see you made it to school."

Alexander nodded.

She turned to Rip. "Take a seat. Now." Rip shot Alexander a mean look. Then he sat down. Alexander breathed a sigh of relief and got in the lunch line.

He grabbed some Taco Surprise and looked for a seat. Most of his classmates were eating together, joking around. The kid in the hoodie sat alone, writing in a notebook.

The notebook, remembered Alexander. He found an empty table, unzipped his backpack, and pulled out the notebook. It was filled with drawings of monsters — hairy birds, eight-eyed mushrooms, mutant earthworms.

He read about flying rhinos while he ate.

RHINOCERAPTOR
An armored beast with a large horn and massive swan-like wings.
HABITAT
Wherever breakable things are kept: china shops, clock museums, violin factories.

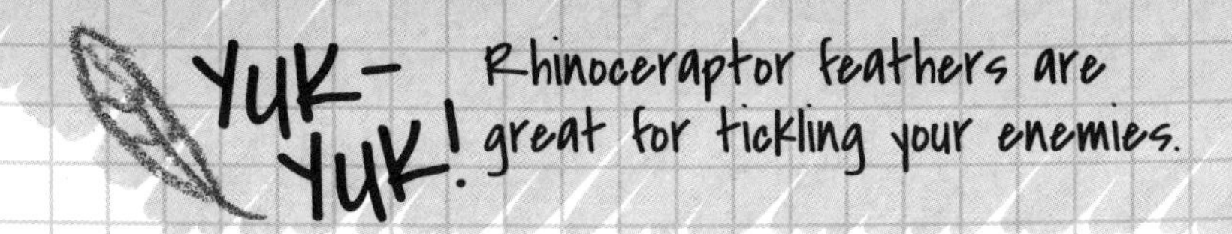

DIET Leafy plants. And corn dogs.

BEHAVIOR These monsters enjoy a peaceful life in the clouds. But if they spot something breakable down below, they immediately dive-bomb their target!

WARNING! Stay calm! The rhinoceraptor can sense fear, so, SERIOUSLY, DON'T FREAK OUT!

The rhinoceraptor won't hurt you, but it'll gladly crush anything you care about—like a fishbowl, a sand castle, Mr. Nuzzle Bear, or a picture of your mom.

Alexander finished his lunch and closed the notebook, bumping his milk carton. It was 2% milk, but 98% of it splashed onto his pants. He began dabbing milk off his pants with his napkin. Then he paused mid-dab.

There was a message on his napkin.

It looked like the message had been signed. But the name had been smudged by spilled milk.

Alexander felt a hard slap on his back.

"Hey, Salamander," said Rip, pulling up a seat.

Alexander jammed the notebook into his backpack. "Stop calling me that!" he said.

"What are you trying to hide?" asked Rip. His hand shot down into Alexander's backpack.

"That's mine!" said Alexander.

Rip smiled. "What's this?" He pulled out a baby-blue party invitation:

"Hey, everybody!" Rip announced. "Salamander Snott is having a birthday party tomorrow! Looks like he's turning two!"

"No!" Alexander stood up. But then he remembered the wet spot on his pants. He sat back down.

Rip marched around the lunchroom, holding up the card.

Alexander felt a gentle pat on his back.

"Here —" said a girl's voice.

It was the kid in the hoodie. She wore the hoodie pulled way, way down. But Alexander could see she had friendly eyes.

"For your pants," she said. She handed him a paper towel. "Hey, I saw your notebook earlier. I keep —"

A buzzer sounded from the loudspeaker.

“Er, hello, students,” said a voice. “This is Mr. Hoarsely. School has been cancelled.”

“Yeah!” shouted Rip as he high-fived a kindergartner on the head.

The speaker crackled again. “The tires have gone flat on all the school buses. Ms. Vanderpants has called off afternoon classes today so you have plenty of time to walk home.”

Everyone looked to the teachers’ table. Mr. Plunkett was clapping.

“Flat tires on every bus?” he said. “Now, *that’s* a prank!”

The students filed out of the cafeteria. Everyone was excited to be walking home on their own. Everyone except for the filthy, tired, frog-booted kid with wet pants.

CHAPTER 9

MONSTERS BEFORE BED

Alexander watched his classmates head off in different directions. The hoodie girl was nowhere to be seen. *Could she have slipped me that note?* he wondered.

On his walk home, Alexander saw one balloon goon — an orange cactus. A group of older kids walked right past it. The balloon danced around, but they didn't seem to notice.

Was I really attacked *by balloons this morning?* thought Alexander. *Maybe the monsters in that weird notebook are getting to me.*

Alexander couldn't wait to look more at the notebook. He hurried the rest of the way to his new home: a small yellow house on the edge of town, near Gobbler's Woods.

"I'm home!" called Alexander. He kicked off his mismatched shoes.

His dad was unpacking dishes. "How'd it go?" he asked.

"Um, okay," Alexander said.

Alexander ate dinner and got ready for bed. It felt good to wash up and change into clean pajamas. He climbed onto his air mattress and, at last, brought out the notebook.

What could S.S.M.P. stand for? he wondered. *And these monsters . . . are they just some kid's doodles? Or could they mean something?* He read another entry.

FORKUPINE

A small metal rodent
with a coat of tiny, sharp forks.

HABITAT Most forkupines prefer dry climates. But the stainless-steel forkupine can be found near rivers, lakes, or in the back of dishwashers.

CLANG! Magnets will not work on forkupines.

DIET

Mostly pickles and olives. They'll eat steak, but only if it's cut up into small bites.

BEHAVIOR

The forkupine stays sharp by rubbing against a brick wall.

WARNING!

Never pet a forkupine! Instead, lure it to a plate of spaghetti. (Forkupines LOVE rolling around in noodles!) This will give you time to sneak away.

FUN FACT

The forkupine is a distant cousin to the sporkupine. But the sporkupine's scoop attack is no match for the forkupine's jab.

"Okay, kiddo, lights out!" Alexander's dad peeked in the door. "Big day tomorrow! I can't wait to see who comes to your party!"

"Uh . . . me neither," said Alexander. He faked a yawn and let his blanket fall onto his backpack, still full of invitations.

CHAPTER 10 ~~HAPPY~~ BIRTHDAY

"Urggghh!" Alexander woke up with a sore back. His air mattress was flat. *Like the dodgeball*, he thought. *And the tires . . .*

Alexander's dad was outside, singing at the top of his lungs.

Alexander looked out the window. His jaw dropped.

HAPPY BIRTHDAY TOOOOO YOUUU!!!

BOPP

His front yard was full of balloon goons! Every size, every color. All of them grinning up at Alexander.

His dad was in the middle of the group, singing like a rock star.

Alexander waved his arms. "Dad! No! Get out of there!" he cried.

His dad looked around, confused. "What?"

"THOSE . . . GOONS! THEY'RE GONNA GET YOU!"

His dad laughed. "Oh, Al, there's nothing to be afraid of. I called Party Planet yesterday to rent something fun for your birthday — it's set up out back! And then this morning, these balloons were waiting in our yard. The store must have thrown them in for free!"

"Those things are monsters!" Alexander shouted.

Alexander's dad sighed. "Al, they're not monsters." He strolled through the yard, bopping balloon goons. He even stopped to honk one on the nose.

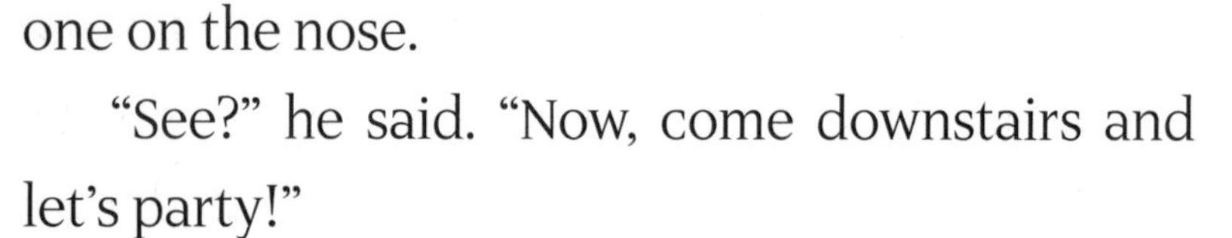

"See?" he said. "Now, come downstairs and let's party!"

Alexander got dressed and headed downstairs.

At first glance, Alexander thought his dad had turned the backyard into a birthday wonderland.

But then Alexander noticed the melting ice cream, the droopy party balloons, and a nervous clown. *Yikes!* thought Alexander. *Good thing I didn't actually invite anyone to this party!* Even the main attraction — a bouncy castle — looked like a smooshed tent.

"Hmmm," said Alexander's dad. "That castle was fully inflated a minute ago. Maybe it's got a leak. . . . I'll check it out. You go on and say hello to your friend."

Friend? thought Alexander. He turned to see a square-headed kid carefully making his way through the front yard. The one person to show up at his party: Rip Bonkowski.

Alexander frowned and walked toward Rip.

CHAPTER 11 A REAL TWIST

"All right, Rip, get it over with," Alexander said. "Throw something at me or call me names or whatever, so you can go home."

"Sounds like fun," Rip said, "but that's not why I'm here. I actually came to tell you" — he slurped some punch — "that I believe you. About the monsters."

Alexander was speechless.

"Did you *hear* me?" asked Rip.

"So, wait," Alexander said. "Are *you* the one who wrote on my napkin yesterday?"

Rip looked confused. "Napkin? No. I thought you were nutso then. But as I was walking home from school, I passed by one of those balloon things. A big orange cactus. It gave me a funny look, so I started throwin' rocks at it. It caught one of my rocks and threw it back at me! Look!"

Rip rolled up his sleeve. There was an ugly red scrape between some of his fake tattoos.

"Whoa," said Alexander.

"Yeah," said Rip. "And then the thing started chasing me! I ran home. I tried to tell my parents, but they didn't believe me. I still had your stupid invitation in my pocket, and I remembered what you'd said in class. So I came here."

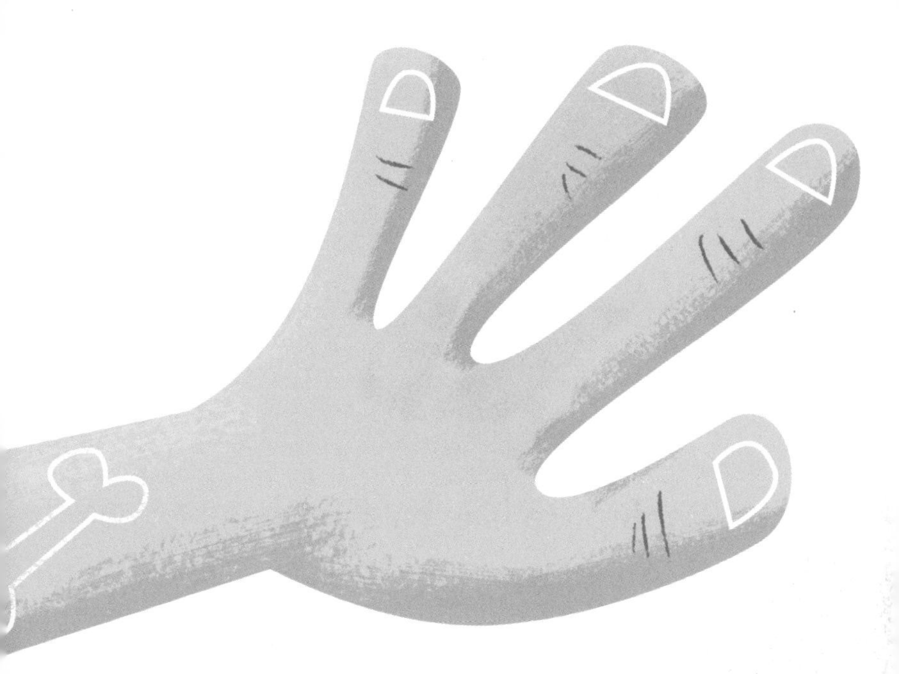

Rip rolled his sleeve back down. “Your front yard is *crawling* with those things! I had to sneak around them.”

“Who can we tell about the balloon goons?” said Alexander.

They looked at the two grown-ups at the party: Alexander’s dad, who was fussing with the bouncy castle, and the nervous clown.

“Let’s try the clown,” Alexander said.

Alexander and Rip walked over to the clown.

The clown wore a fake bald cap and big, pointy shoes. A smile was painted on his face, but he didn't look happy. He was blowing up a balloon.

"Excuse me," said Alexander.

"Eep!" The clown released his balloon. He glanced at the woods, then back at the boys. "Pay attention!" he said. "I'm about to show you a very important balloon animal."

"Um, okay . . ." said Alexander.

The clown blew up a long, skinny balloon.

"Now watch!" He held the balloon by one end and twisted the other end around. "Left, right, left. Down, around, pull!"

He gave the balloon one last tug. "Ta-daaa!"

"What is it?" asked Alexander. "One big knot?"

"No — a mangled pretzel!" said Rip.

The clown wiped his brow. "Just remember: left, right, left. Down, around —"

"Hi, boys!" Alexander's dad jumped out from behind a shrub.

"Eep!" the clown shrieked, dropping his balloon knot. The balloon popped and the clown shrieked again.

Alexander's dad laughed. "This guy's a hoot!"

"Yeah, he's crazy all right," said Alexander, peering into the woods.

CHAPTER 12 CLOWNING AROUND

"I've got terrible news," said Alexander's dad. "I can't get this bouncy castle all the way aired up."

He pointed to a poster on a nearby tree. "But here's something even better: Pin the Tail on the Donkey!" He held up a cardboard tail attached to a long, sharp pin.

"That looks dangerous!" said the clown, taking a step back.

Alexander's dad removed his tie. "Nope!" he said. "Here. Blindfold me — I'll show you!"

The nervous clown tied the blindfold. Then Alexander's dad spun around three times. He smiled and began marching in a straight line . . . away from the donkey.

“Dad —” Alexander said.

“I can do this!” his dad said. “Watch the master.”

Alexander, Rip, and the clown all watched Alexander’s dad walk across the backyard and around the corner of the garage.

The clown tugged nervously on his suspenders. “Maybe we should practice more balloon animals until your dad comes back.”

Rip elbowed Alexander in the ribs. “Tell him, Salamander.”

“Um, Mr. Clown,” said Alexander, “you know those balloons in my front yard?”

“Yes?” he said.

“I know this sounds crazy,” Alexander said, “but Rip and I” — he leaned in — “we think they’re alive. They’re monsters!”

"I believe you, Alexander. I'm the one who wrote on your napkin."

"Huh?" said Alexander. "Wait, *you* were at the cafeteria?"

The clown looked straight at the boys. "And even if I didn't believe you before," he whispered, "*Ummm* . . . Turn. Around. Slowly."

Alexander and Rip turned. A white balloon goon was dragging itself along the ground. It was floppier than the others.

The clown's makeup turned two shades paler.

"Their secret is in these woods, behind your house." The clown was backing away. "They'll do anything to protect it. RUN FOR YOUR LIVES!"

Alexander watched as the clown jumped out of his shoes and ran, faster than any clown has ever run from a balloon.

CHAPTER 13 PSSSHHHHHH!

The white balloon goon lurched toward the two boys.

"Rip, run!" Alexander shouted.

"No," Rip said. "It's just a balloon." He picked up a giant clown shoe. "I say we fight."

Alexander scrambled onto the picnic table.

The balloon goon opened a large valve on the bouncy castle. Air rushed out with a great **PSSSHHHHHH!** The goon chomped on the valve, swelling up from the escaping air.

"It's eating the air," Rip said.

"It all makes sense now!" yelled Alexander. "The flat tires, the dodgeball, my mattress — these goons have been stealing air from everything in town!"

The balloon goon had doubled in size. It had four wiggly arms, all reaching for Rip.

Rip held the floppy shoe like a baseball bat. "You don't scare me."

The goon scrunched down like a spring and then vaulted toward Rip. Rip swung the pointy-toed shoe with both hands — **SPLACK!** — making a tear in the goon's silky belly. The monster collapsed as the air whooshed out of its wound.

Alexander shouted down to Rip. "You did it!"

Rip twirled the shoe on the end of his finger. "Of course I did, Salamander."

Then one hundred more balloon goons came to the party.

CHAPTER 14 BOUNCING OFF THE WALLS

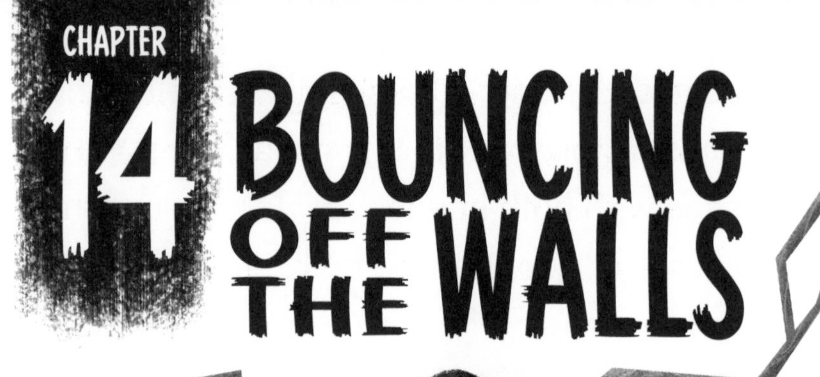

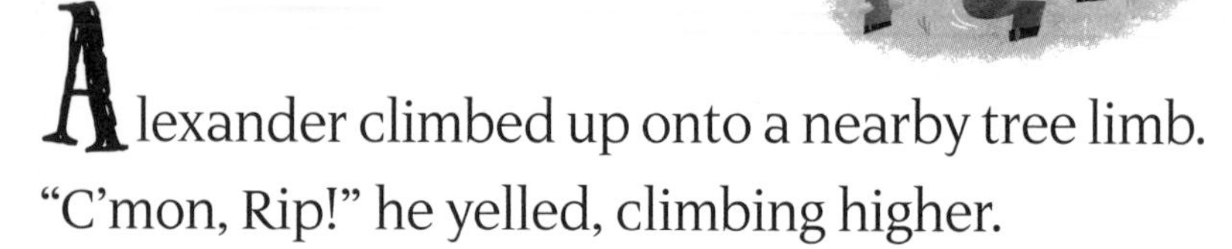

Alexander climbed up onto a nearby tree limb. "C'mon, Rip!" he yelled, climbing higher.

Balloon goons filled the backyard. The group from the front circled around the house as dozens more glided in from the woods. The crowd of swaying monsters silently zeroed in on Rip.

"No way!" said Rip.

He swung his clown shoe but was no match for the balloons. They grabbed Rip and lifted him high in the air.

"Salamander! Help!" he shouted.

Alexander hugged his branch as the balloons carried Rip off into the woods.

A moment later, Alexander dropped from the tree.

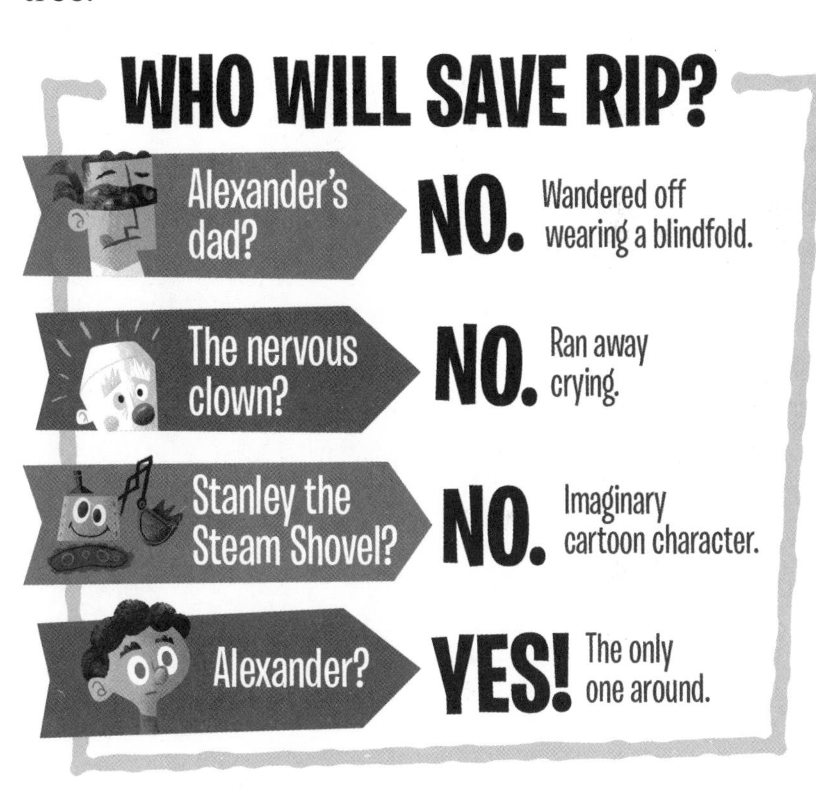

Alexander trailed the balloon goons as they marched through the woods. Then he gasped.

Before him stood the largest bouncy castle ever built! It was the size of a real castle, with towers, battlements — even a drawbridge. Except the entire thing was made of rubber.

The balloon goons dragged Rip into their bouncy fortress, leaving the drawbridge open.

Alexander stepped onto the drawbridge. It wobbled slightly. He took a breath and entered the gate.

It was dark inside. Alexander could hear a faint **SHHH-SHHHHH** sound, as though the walls were breathing. There was no sign of Rip or any balloon goons.

Walking was tricky, so Alexander tried jumping. The springy floor launched him up to the ceiling. He rebounded off a wall and bounced down the hallway.

Alexander bopped his way through the maze of passageways. He got lost a few times but eventually found himself in the heart of the fortress. It was an enormous room with no ceiling — just the blue morning sky.

In the middle of the arena, a kid was tied to an inflatable post.

Alexander leaped over. "Rip! You're alive!"

Rip smiled. "Salamander! Untie me!"

Alexander worked at the knots. "Why did they bring you to their fortress?"

"Fortress?" Rip snorted. "This place is a *factory*! While you were

playing hopscotch, they brought out a million baby balloon goons and forced me to blow 'em up. Once I ran out of breath, they tied me up."

"Is that their secret?" Alexander asked. "They're building an army?" He loosened one knot, but there were dozens to go. "Just imagine: no pool toys! No bikes! And" — he swallowed — "no whoopee cushions! We *have* to stop them."

The ground began to quiver. Alexander heard a low rumbling, like hundreds of basketballs being dribbled at once. An army of angry balloon goons swarmed in from all sides.

The boys were surrounded.

CHAPTER

15 READY OR KNOT

"Hold still!" said Alexander.

"It's no use," said Rip. "There are too many knots!"

More balloon goons were pouring into the room. Alexander had to think fast. He jumped straight up, came back down, and then bounced higher. He came down a second time and a third, until he shot up above the tallest goons. They wobbled in place, their eyes fixed on the leaping boy. Alexander bounced higher yet. From way up there, the goons looked small — harmless, even.

"Heads up!" shouted Rip.

Alexander saw the green OUR DUST balloon from the corner of his eye. It twirled something on the end of a string and let it fly.

O R DUST

WHAP!

Alexander was hit by his old shoe, and began to fall. He hugged his knees and cannonballed into the crowd. He slammed down onto the green balloon goon.

That goon exploded, releasing a blast of air that knocked the rest of the goons to the floor.

"That," said Rip, "was amazing."

Alexander shakily stood up. "We can take 'em. One at a time, they're not very strong."

"Uh-oh . . ." said Rip. "Look!"

The floored balloon goons were crawling toward one another like inchworms. They began twisting their bodies together and had soon braided themselves into one gigantic balloon snake.

The massive snake reared its head high, casting a shadow on the boys.

CHAPTER

16 THE POINT

Alexander's eyes grew wide as the giant balloon snake towered overhead.

"So. About these knots —" said Rip. **FWISH!** The snake wrapped itself around him.

Knots, thought Alexander. His eyes lit up. "Rip, don't move."

"No problem," Rip squeaked.

"Hey, airhead!" Alexander shouted at the snake.

The snake turned to face Alexander. Then it attacked!

Alexander bounced to the left, dodging the snake's head.

He frog-hopped around the arena, changing direction with each leap.

"Left! Right! Left!" he shouted. The snake followed Alexander's lead.

Alexander sprung off a wall and flew behind the snake. "Down! Around!"

Finally, he landed near the snake's tail and rocketed straight up. "PULL!"

The snake's head shot through its own coils, stretching its body tight. Its huge jaws snapped at Alexander but missed. He fell to the ground and then looked up. The snake had let go of Rip. It had tied itself into a knot — a giant copy of the clown's balloon animal!

The snake began twisting about, trying to untangle itself. But the more it struggled, the tighter it squeezed, until . . .

BLAM!

. . . it exploded into a shower of confetti.

Alexander ran over to untie Rip. Then the two boys bounced their way out of the fortress.

Rip looked at the mop-haired, bug-eyed, gut-filled bag of bones that had saved his life. "Thanks, Alexander."

Alexander grinned. "My friends call me Salamander."

"You know," Rip said, "anyone brave enough to take on an army of —"

SSSSHHHHHH! The boys turned around. The bouncy fortress had sprouted arms, legs, wings, and a long, spiky tail. It had turned into a huge balloon dragon!

The dragon charged at the boys.

AAAAAHH!

POP!

The dragon zoomed up into the sky like the world's loudest whoopee cushion. A blindfolded man stood where the balloon dragon had been. He was holding a long, sharp pin.

"Did I win?" asked Alexander's dad. He peeked under his blindfold. "Nuts! Not even close!"

The boys laughed. "I could really go for some cake," said Alexander.

They hiked back to the party. Alexander's dad studied the donkey poster while the boys headed to the picnic table. They found the clown hiding underneath. His bald cap had fallen off, revealing a shock of white hair.

"Mr. Hoarsely!" Alexander said. "*You* passed me that note?"

"Boys — you're not dead!?!" said Mr. Hoarsely.

Rip flexed his muscles. Alexander rolled his eyes.

Mr. Hoarsely climbed out from underneath the table. "Does this mean you know about the *other* monsters?" he asked.

Rip looked around. "Other monsters?"

"Hang on!" Alexander ran inside and brought out the notebook.

Mr. Hoarsely trembled. "How did you find *that*?" He leaned in. "Yes. As you can see, those balloons were only the beginning. If you're smart, you'll —" He looked up.

Alexander's dad was standing there.

Mr. Hoarsely shook Alexander's dad's hand. "Thanks for hiring Clowns-to-Go. Gotta go!" He gave the boys a serious look. They could tell he had more to say, but that it would have to wait.

"What did he mean by 'only the beginning'?" Rip asked.

Alexander whispered, "Can you keep a secret?" He handed the monster-filled notebook to his new friend.

Rip flipped through a few pages. "These monsters aren't scary," he said.

Alexander poked Rip's shoulder. "Before today, would you have thought *balloons* could be scary?"

"Good point," said Rip. "Hey, why are there empty pages in the back?"

Alexander held up a pencil. "I think I know." He turned to the first empty page and began to write. . . .

BALLOON GOON

A tall, wiggly creature that is full of air. Most people pass right by these monsters without giving them a second glance.

HABITAT Balloon goons dance in front of used-car lots, diners, and construction sites. They sometimes build balloon fortresses where they can hang out.

SHHH!
Balloon goons are totally silent creatures.
DIET
A balloon goon eats air that it steals from things like footballs, whoopee cushions, and air mattresses.
BEHAVIOR
An army of balloon goons can twist together to form a giant balloony snake monster!
WARNING!
Carry a pin if you think a balloon goon is nearby. They'll really get the point!

TROY CUMMINGS

has no tail, no wings, no fangs, no claws, and only one head. As a kid, he believed that monsters might really exist. Today, he's sure of it.

BEHAVIOR This creature tromps around until way past midnight, writing books, designing jigsaw puzzles, and drawing birthday cards.

HABITAT Troy Cummings lives in Greencastle, Indiana, with his wife and hatchlings.

DIET Malted milk balls.

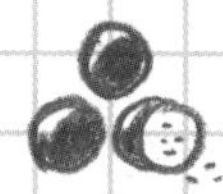

EVIDENCE Few people believe that Troy Cummings is real. The only proof we have is that he supposedly wrote and illustrated The Eensy Weensy Spider Freaks Out! and Giddy-up, Daddy!

WARNING! Keep your eyes peeled for more danger in The Notebook of Doom #2:

DAY OF THE NIGHT CRAWLERS